This Little Tiger book
belongs to:

_____

_____

_____

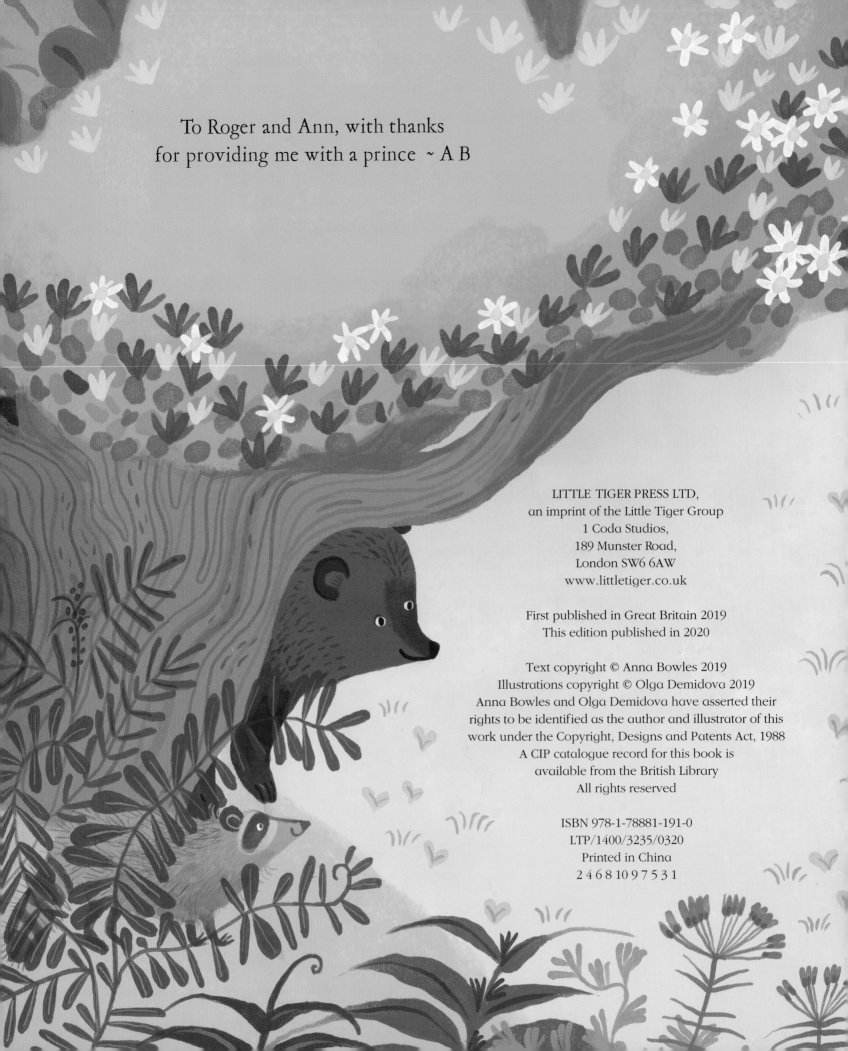

To Roger and Ann, with thanks
for providing me with a prince ~ A B

LITTLE TIGER PRESS LTD,
an imprint of the Little Tiger Group
1 Coda Studios,
189 Munster Road,
London SW6 6AW
www.littletiger.co.uk

First published in Great Britain 2019
This edition published in 2020

Text copyright © Anna Bowles 2019
Illustrations copyright © Olga Demidova 2019
Anna Bowles and Olga Demidova have asserted their
rights to be identified as the author and illustrator of this
work under the Copyright, Designs and Patents Act, 1988
A CIP catalogue record for this book is
available from the British Library
All rights reserved

ISBN 978-1-78881-191-0
LTP/1400/3235/0320
Printed in China
2 4 6 8 10 9 7 5 3 1

FAIRYTALE CLASSICS

Snow White
and the Seven Dwarfs

Anna Bowles

Olga Demidova

LITTLE TIGER

LONDON

It was the coldest night of the
coldest winter there had ever been.
The Queen watched the snow falling.
It was so beautiful that she forgot her
sewing. As she picked it up again . . .

Ouch!

Soon afterwards the Queen gave birth to a daughter called **Snow White.**

The baby was lovely but sadly the poor Queen died. The King took a new wife. She was beautiful, but vain and mean-hearted.

Every morning the new Queen would ask her magic mirror:

Mirror, mirror on the wall, Who is the fairest of them all?

"You, my Queen, are the fairest of them all," the mirror would reply.

But one day it said:

"You, my Queen, are fair, it's true. But Snow White is a hundred times fairer than you."

The Queen threw a fit! She ran to find Snow White.
It was true! The girl was the fairest ever born.

Take her!

"Huntsman!" she ordered. "Take Snow White
into the forest and kill her!"

But the huntsman was a good man.

He let her run away.

As Snow White wandered
afraid in the forest, she
came across a little house.

The door was unlocked.
Snow White peeped inside.
A table was laid with
seven little plates.

Snow White was
hungry and thirsty.

She ate and ate.
She drank and
she drank.

Then upstairs
Snow White found
seven little beds.

Finally she fell fast asleep.
    The house belonged to seven dwarfs.
When they came home they had a
BIG surprise!

Someone's eaten MY food!

Someone's drunk up MY water!

When Snow White woke up in the morning,
she told the dwarfs who she was.

That sounded like a lot of work,
but what else was she to do?

That same morning, the
Queen asked:

"Mirror, mirror, on the wall,
Who is the fairest of them all?"

"You my Queen, are fair, it's true.
But Snow White is a **thousand**
times fairer than you."

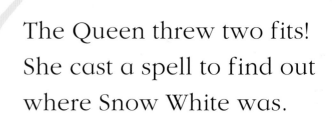

The Queen threw two fits!
She cast a spell to find out
where Snow White was.

Then she disguised
herself as an old woman
selling trinkets.

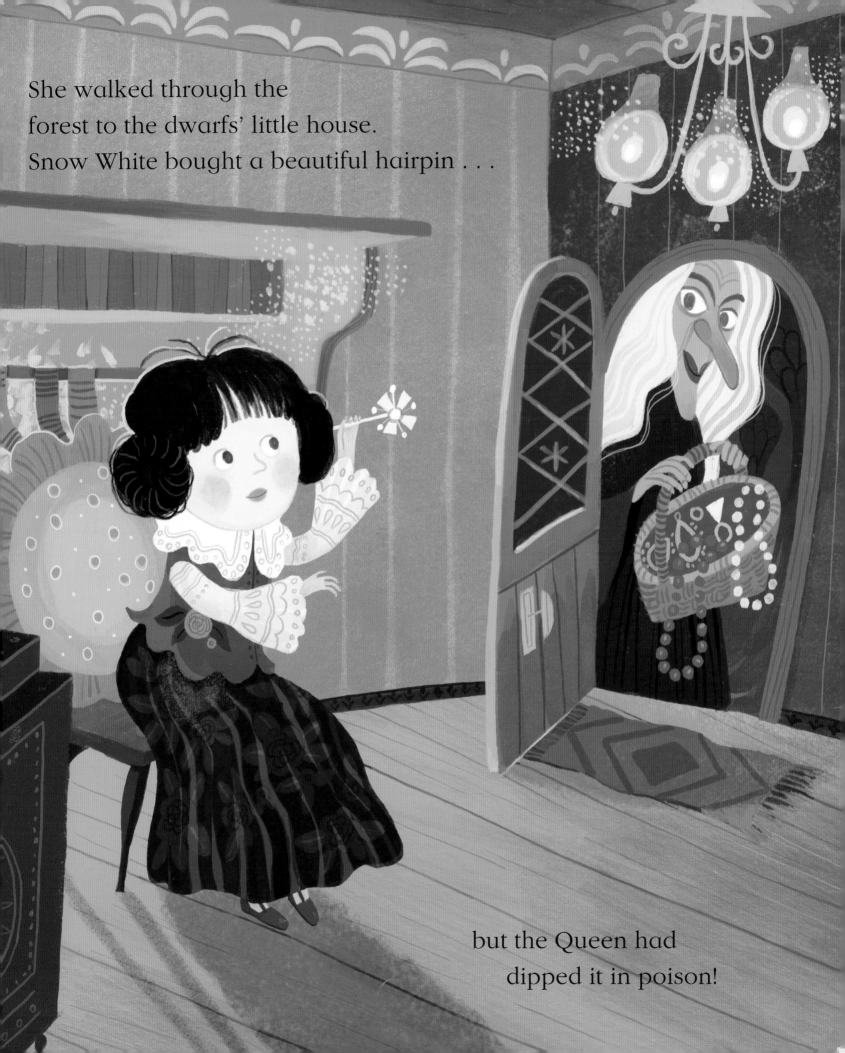

She walked through the
forest to the dwarfs' little house.
Snow White bought a beautiful hairpin . . .

but the Queen had
dipped it in poison!

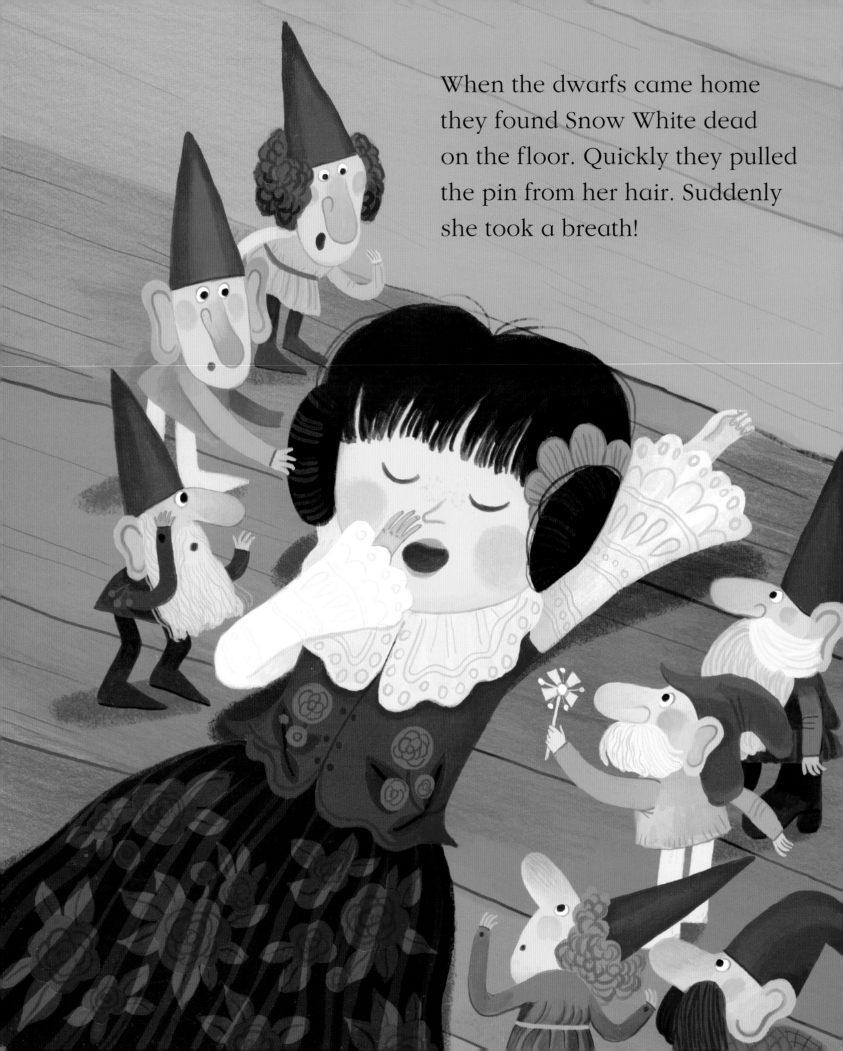

When the dwarfs came home they found Snow White dead on the floor. Quickly they pulled the pin from her hair. Suddenly she took a breath!

Back at the palace,
the Queen asked:

Once again the
mirror replied,

*"You, my Queen,
are fair, it's true.
But Snow White is
a million times
fairer than you!"*

Mirror, mirror
on the wall,
Who is the fairest
of them all?

The Queen threw two fits and
was about to throw another but
she realised it wouldn't help.

Instead she found an apple,
filled it with poison and
hurried into the forest.

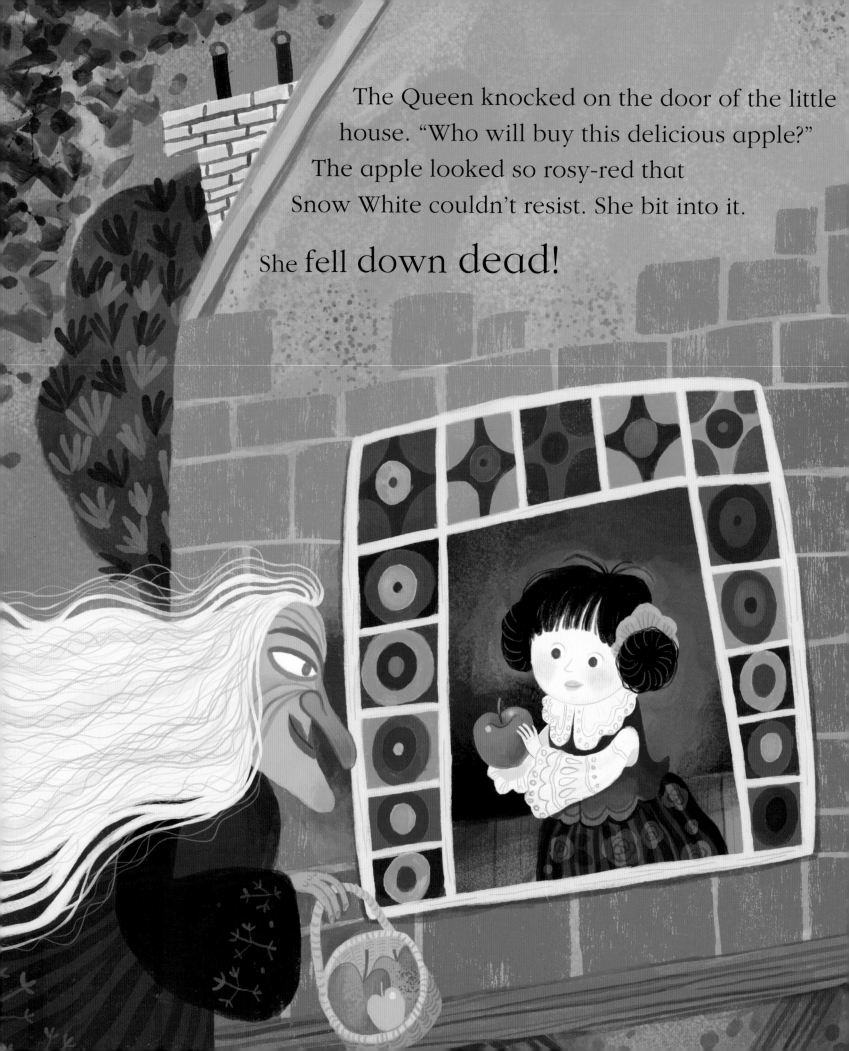

The Queen knocked on the door of the little house. "Who will buy this delicious apple?" The apple looked so rosy-red that Snow White couldn't resist. She bit into it.

She fell down dead!

Once again, the Queen asked:

"*Mirror, mirror, on the wall,*
Who is the fairest of them all?"
"*You, my Queen, are the fairest of all.*"

Finally!

Although Snow White was dead, her body stayed beautiful.
The poor dwarfs wept for a day and a night.
Then they made a wonderful glass coffin for
her and placed it on the mountainside.

All the birds and beasts could see how lovely Snow White was. For a year and a day, they watched over her.

One morning, men came riding by. Their bells jingled and their spurs jangled, for they were the fine men and fine horses of Prince Harold.

What's this?

The heart-broken dwarfs told him their tale.

"Alas," said the Prince. He leant over
Snow White's coffin to give her a single kiss.

Snow White woke up!

But when the evil Queen questioned the mirror again, it replied:

"You, my Queen are fair, it's true.
But Snow White is fairer,
and gentler and kinder,
*so everyone **loves her**, not you!"*

The Queen was so angry that she went up in a Puff of smoke!

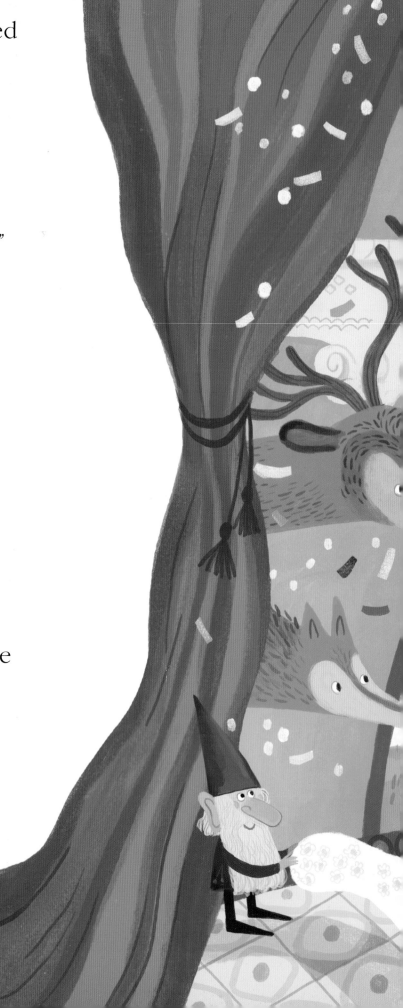

And the Prince and Snow White were soon married and lived happily ever after.

FAIRYTALE CLASSICS

are familiar, fun and friendly stories – with a marvellously modern twist!

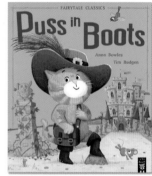

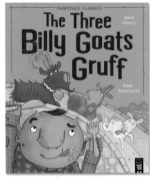

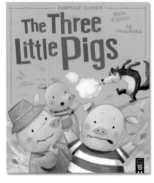

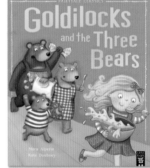

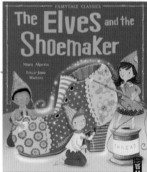

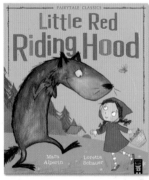

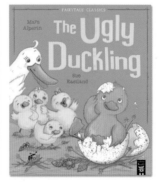

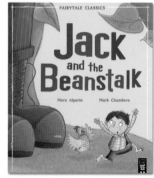

For information regarding any of the above titles or for our catalogue, please contact us:
Little Tiger Press Ltd, 1 Coda Studios, 189 Munster Road, London SW6 6AW
Tel: 020 7385 6333 • E-mail: contact@littletiger.co.uk • www.littletiger.co.uk